THE
UGLIEST
DOG
IN THE WORLD

BRUCE WHATLEY

For Rosie, Ben and Ellyn
with special thanks to Skitty
the best dog in the world

Angus&Robertson
An imprint of HarperCollins*Publishers*, Australia

First published in Australia in 1992
This edition 1995

HarperCollins*Publishers*
25 Ryde Road, Pymble, Sydney, NSW 2073, Australia
Distributed in the US by HarperCollins World
10 East 53rd Street, New York NY 10022-5299, USA

National Library of Australia Cataloguing-in-Publication data:

Whatley, Bruce.
The ugliest dog in the world.
ISBN 0 207 18768 1.
1. Dogs – Juvenile fiction. I. Title.
A823'.2

Printed in Hong Kong

8 7 6 5 4 3 2 1   95 96 97 98 99

THE
UGLIEST
DOG
IN THE WORLD

BRUCE WHATLEY

Angus&Robertson
An imprint of HarperCollinsPublishers

Everybody sees
my dog differently.

My dad thinks she is
the ugliest dog in the world.

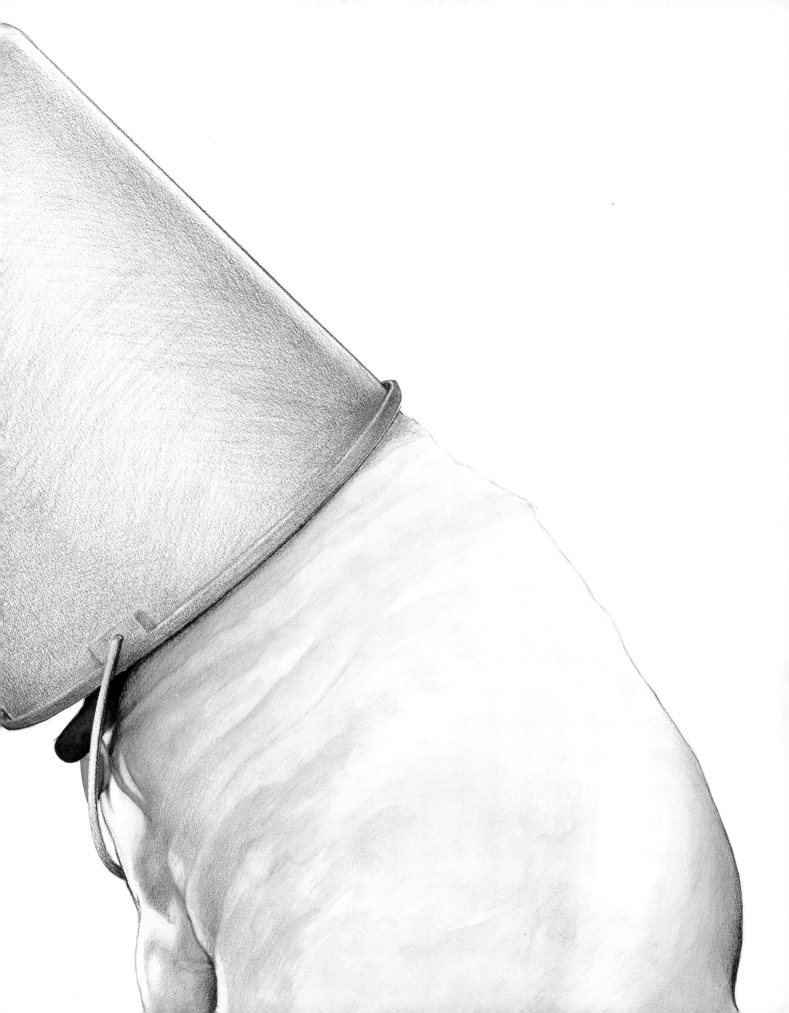

My mom thinks she's ugly too
but in a cute sort of way.

The lady next door
actually thinks she's pretty.
But you haven't seen
the lady next door!

Even Gran thinks she's ugly.
It's funny though, she laughs
every time she sees her.

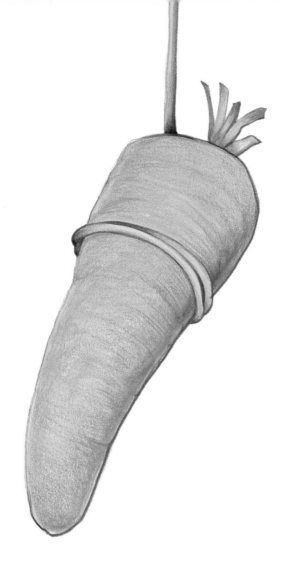

Grandpa thinks
she's shy and stubborn,
but it gets ugly when he tries
to take her for a walk.

Little Sammy,
who wants to be a fireman
when he grows up,
thinks she's a bit of a drip.

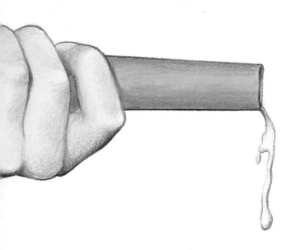

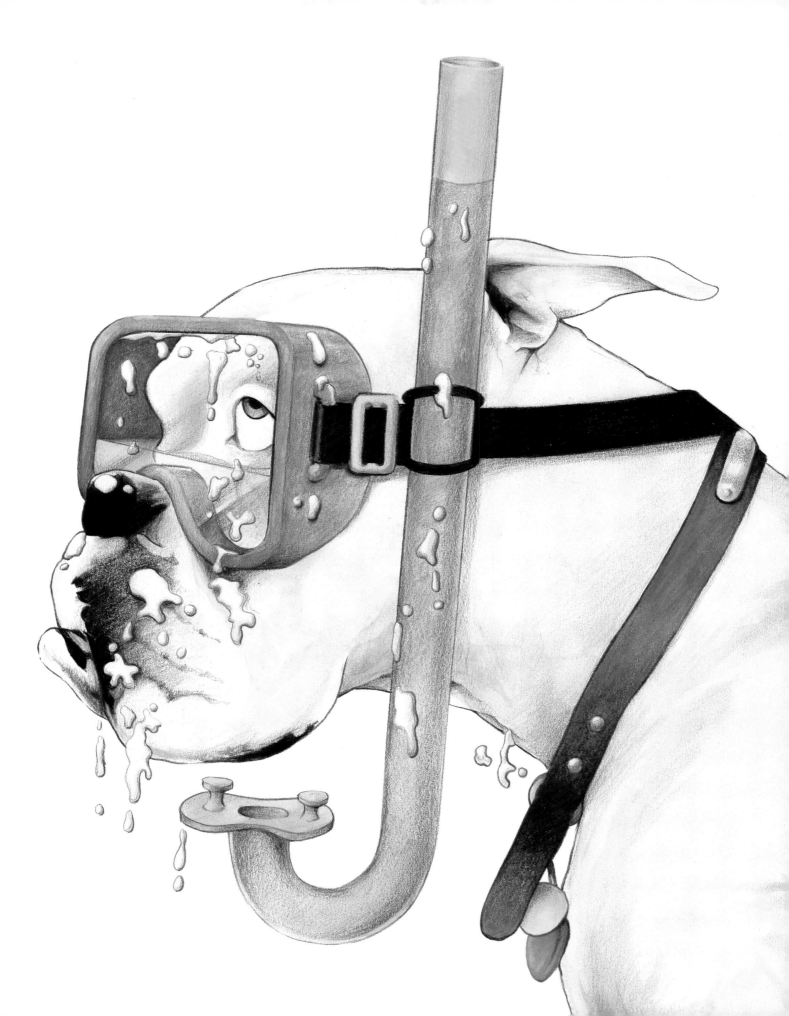

The butcher thinks she's
all beef and no brains.
I think he spends
too much time in his shop.

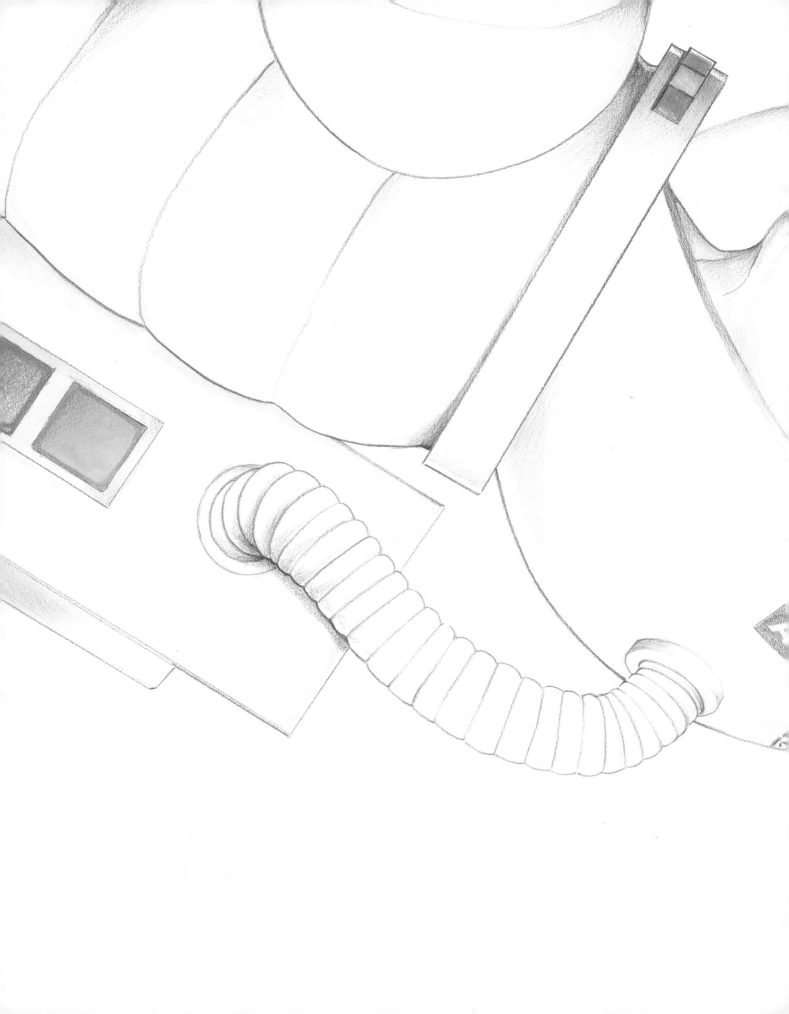

The postman just thinks she's ugly
and would like to send her far away.

Auntie Nellie thinks she's ugly too
— in a crazy kind of way.

My brother thinks she's really ugly.
He says she's a monster
and chases her
all around the house.

The police think that
she looks like a criminal
and if she could drive
a get-away car
she'd rob banks.

My teacher thinks she has
the classic features of an ancient ruin.
In other words — she's ugly!

My best friend thinks she's ugly.
She SCREAMS whenever
she sees her!

But I love my dog.
I think she's beautiful...

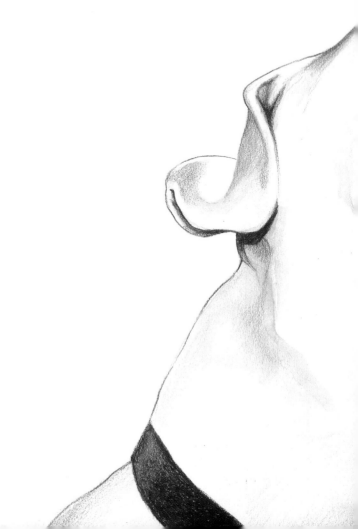

in a sloppy kind of way!